First published in Belgium and Holland by Clavis Uitgeverij, Hasselt – Amsterdam, 2010
Copyright © 2010, Clavis Uitgeverij

English translation from the Dutch by Clavis Publishing Inc. New York
Copyright © 2010 for the English language edition: Clavis Publishing Inc. New York

Visit us on the web at www.clavisbooks.com

Lucky's Little Feather written and illustrated by Peggy van Gurp
Original title: *Geluksveertje*
Translated from the Dutch by Clavis Publishing

ISBN 978-1-60537-086-6

This book was printed in july 2010 at Ozgraf, Olsztynskie Zaklady Graficzne SA in UI. Towarowa 2, PL-10-417 Olsztyn, Poland
First Edition
10 9 8 7 6 5 4 3 2 1

Peggy van Gurp

Lucky's Little Feather

Clavis

NEW YORK

"Hi Lucky. What have you got there?"
"Hi Lucy. This is a little lucky feather."
"A lucky feather? You're kidding me!"
"No, really, it's a lucky feather."

"When I found this little feather yesterday and tried to pick it up,
the wind blew it right in front of me into a small hole.
I ran after it and climbed into the hole.
Lucky me, because right at that moment a fox trotted by.
If I hadn't been hiding in that little hole, that fox surely would have eaten me."
"That's a coincidence, Lucky."
"No, it's good luck."

"Then I ran home, because it started to rain very hard.
WHACK, WHACK, WHACK, thick raindrops pattered on the floor.
Since I was in a hurry, I didn't look where I was going.
I fell down with my nose in the mud."
"That's bad luck, Lucky."
"No, it's good luck, because my feather stayed completely clean."

"When I was almost home, a thunderstorm burst out
and a big branch fell down.
BANG, right on top of my house."
"Oh no, that's terrible!"
"No, it's good luck. I wasn't inside my hole,
because I wasn't home yet."

"Luckily, I soon found a new place to sleep.
I slept in the small hole in which the wind had blown my lucky feather.
When I ran out this morning, I accidentally dropped my little feather."
"Oh dear, what a pity!"
"No, it's good luck, because right at that time an eagle flew down to snatch me.
The bird couldn't catch me, because I was bending down to pick up my lucky feather."

"Look, I only have a little scratch."
"Ouch, that looks painful!"

"No, it's good luck. It could have been much worse.
Imagine if the eagle had caught me …"

"Instead, I am here with you.
Talking about my little lucky feather."

At that moment the little feather is blown away.
Lucky and Lucy can grab it just in time.
"Bad luck, Lucky!"
"No, it's good luck. Look up."

Lucky and Lucy land in the eagle's nest.
"Oh dear, what now, Lucky?"

"Come on, Lucy, hold on tight.
We'll float down with my little feather."

"Give me your hand, Lucy.
Now we're down on the ground and we are safe.
We have been so lucky!"

"Now do you believe it's a lucky feather?
Here you are, Lucy, the little feather is yours."

"Oh, thank you, Lucky!
That's so sweet of you."

"Maybe your little feather does bring good luck."